The Artist
and the King

JULIE FORTENBERRY

Alazar Press   Carrboro, NC

Thank you to the artists who helped me
write this story, especially Kathleen O'Dell.

Copyright © 2014 Julie Fortenberry. All rights reserved.
Library of Congress Control Number: 2013912525
ISBN 978-0-9793000-3-5
Design and production by Julie Allred, BW&A Books, Inc.
Edited by Jacqueline K. Ogburn

www.alazar-press.com

First printing. Printed in China.
Printing Plant Location: Printed by
    Everbest Printing Co. Ltd.,
    Nansha, China
Production Date: July 24, 2013
Job/Batch #: 113415

On the day of the royal parade, the weather was calm, but for one short gust of wind that picked up a little girl's painting . . .

and slapped it over the King's face.

"Who did this?" yelled the King.

"My name is Daphne.
I am the artist, your majesty."

"Artist?" cried the King.
"Give me your artist's cap.
From this day forward,
you'll wear a dunce cap instead.
Artist! Ha!"

He rolled up her painting
and stuck it on her head.

She should have felt lucky.
After all, her punishment was just a silly hat.
She'd heard about other people who were banished
by the King. Sent far from friends and family,
they were never allowed to come home.

But Daphne didn't feel lucky. She felt ridiculous,
and she missed her lovely red artist beret.

Was there a way, she wondered,
to make the hat look less duncey?

Maybe if she wore it to one side.

Or under her hair.

She tried adding
colorful decorations.

And with a
piece of fabric,
the cap looked
almost regal!

With the right fabrics, it could
match her different dresses.

Soon she was getting
compliments.

Neighbors and friends asked for caps of their own.

She began selling her caps in the marketplace,
and trading them for exotic ribbons, gems,
feathers and buttons to make new caps.

"She knows just how to pick the perfect cap
to suit any face," said a customer.

"She has such an eye for
color and proportion,"
said another.

Soon they were ordering
custom caps for holidays
or as gifts for loved ones.

Perhaps Daphne was still an artist after all!
Her caps seemed almost magical. The entire town
was a little more colorful, more lively, because of them.

But then the King took notice. "What is this mockery?
Dunce caps are a punishment and only I decide who wears one!"

"Every dunce in a dunce cap into the wilderness!" he cried,
leading his army to the market square.

And straight to his own daughter!

"My dear girl, step aside or be banished with the others."

The Princess threw down a cap.

"As you wish, Father!"

She turned and walked into the woods.

One by one, the others followed.

When the soldiers saw their families going, they followed, leaving the King alone in the market square.

Daphne looked back at that cap, then at the King's spear, hovering directly above it.

That beautiful cap, crumpled in the dirt!

She made a run for it.

But she stopped short.

Was the King crying?

She touched the picture
on her cap. Could it be?
Could she feel sad for
the King?

"I'm sorry I painted that
mean picture of you,"
she said softly.

At that the King grunted, and Daphne thought
he might yell at her again, but instead he said,
"No, little girl. I was the mean one.
Even my daughter said so."

"But your daughter loves you.
Look!" said Daphne.

Sure enough, a note
on the cap said:

For
My Dear Father,
with Love

Now the King was
crying even harder.

"Come now, your majesty," said Daphne.
"We can still bring everyone home."

And so they did.

By morning, even the villagers who had been exiled long ago, were streaming home. The crowd in the marketplace cheered at the sight of each one coming over the hill.

But the loudest cheer was for Daphne.

"Long live Daphne," they cheered.

7/14

11/15 3x last 6/15